THE CHRISTMAS PRINCESS

MARIAH CAREY

and MICHAELA ANGELA DAVIS

illustrated by FUUJI TAKASHI

HENRY HOLT AND COMPANY ✹ NEW YORK

Henry Holt and Company, *Publishers since 1866*
Henry Holt® is a registered trademark of Macmillan Publishing Group, LLC
120 Broadway, New York, NY 10271 • mackids.com

Our books may be purchased in bulk for promotional, educational, or business use.
Please contact your local bookseller or the Macmillan Corporate and Premium Sales Department
at (800) 221-7945 ext. 5442 or by email at MacmillanSpecialMarkets@macmillan.com.

Library of Congress Cataloging-in-Publication Data is available.

First edition, 2022
Book design by Mina Chung
Printed in China by RR Donnelley Asia Printing Solutions Ltd., Dongguan City, Guangdong Province

ISBN 978-1-250-83711-0 (hardcover)

1 3 5 7 9 10 8 6 4 2

Dear Little Mariah,

You are a wonderful, one-of-a-kind wonder! I know you may not feel that way right now because you don't have a "normal" name like Katie or Julie, and most people don't even know how to pronounce Mariah (though it's not even that hard). I know a lot of people put you down because of your clothes, your house, and your hair, and try to make you feel "other"— that they are better than you are and you are less of who you are.

But I want to tell you this truth: no matter what things look like now, you are worthy and deserving of all the attention, love, protection, care, conditioner, and fancy dresses in the whole wide world. I am so proud of how you have held on to your faith, no matter what. And because of your faith and pure heart, you will move past the mean people and get through the scary stuff and will grow up to have more than you or anyone could ever imagine. And you will spread the spirit of Christmas all over the land for all of time.

Love,

Mariah

P.S. Multitudes of people will not only know how to pronounce your name, they will actually name little girls after YOU!

Once, time was upon Little Mariah.
She was too young to tell time, it's true,
but old timey-time was always telling her what to do.

TIME to get up, Ma . . . ri . . . ah!
Pavarotti (aka Mike the Bird), her mother's two-faced, two-toned parrot,
would loudly squawk.
"La, la-la, la, la-la, la-la," Mother (La Diva) sang right after him in her rich
mezzo-soprano voice.
You see, she really preferred not to talk.

Little Mariah, her operatic mother, and the double-dealing bird
lived in a saggy, wobbly, bubbly brick little shack surrounded by a wild wood
at the end of a narrow rocky road.
It was totally misplaced in a fancy neighborhood.

There was a grand white house with black shutters high up on a hill.

The shack sat sadly in the valley below.

It looked like something the big house spit out because it was ill.

It was pretty dreary inside.

The white lace curtains were dusty and dingy;

nothing in there was new.

The walls were warped and wavy,

so all the pictures were slightly askew.

An old bumpy, lumpy, grimy, and grim red carpet
full of fleas covered the creaky, squeaky floor.
A shabby, fidgety, three-legged blue corduroy couch
that rocked faced the lockless door.

In the middle of the rundown dwelling

was an unsteady flight of wooden stairs with rickety rails.

Little Mariah had to watch where she stepped,

and had to beware of pesky little nails,

popping up out of nowhere, snagging her stockings,

pricking her pinkie toe, then snickering when they were done.

Pesky snickering nails in the stairs with rickety rails really was no fun.

One brilliant spot inside the dank shaky shack was an old golden brown
upright piano, elegant, solid, and bright.
Whose black and white keys held all the hopes and possibilities
of music, joy, and light.
Sitting on the bench, humming a marvelous melody written in her mind,
was the one place in the world Little Mariah felt she belonged and was all right.

Ma . . . ri . . . ah! TIME to brush the hair!
Pavarotti, aka Mike the Bird, screeched, perched atop Mother La Diva's head,
displaying his vibrant hues of yellow, blue, and green like a bright balloon.
"La, la-la, la, la-la, la-la," she sang in response in her most dramatic tune.

She'd run and fetch her mother's big silver brush,

which she liked very much.

The bristles were the color of sweet cream and soft to the touch.

Mother La Diva's hair was long and super thick.

Precariously Little Mariah stood on the back of the three-legged couch

to help reach her scalp, because La Diva insisted her luxurious tresses

were flawlessly placed, smooth and slick.

On the other hand, Little Mariah's hair was a wild thick garden
of straight, curly, frizzy, wavy, and wiry strands
with naughty knotty knots underneath, going every which-a-way.
Never, ever was it tended to, nary a detangling moment,
and, of course, she never had a special hair-washing day.

Little Mariah slept in a tiny attic room
with a crooked roof too small to stand up in.
She had so few things to call her own:
her special notebook of songs and Cuddles the teddy bear,
but she never complained about her cramped circumstances.
Besides she was pretty thin.

Little Mariah never wore a coordinating outfit.
She only had three random shirts, one checkered skirt,
some mix-matched striped stockings . . . Yup, that's about it!
Except for some hand-me-down old ankle boots with a hole at the left toe
and her one treasure—a red coat that had once belonged to her beloved Nana.
It had tattered patches and unraveling threads,
but was oh-so cheerful against the glistening white snow.

TIME to clean the birdcage, Ma...ri...ah!
squeaked Pavarotti, aka Mike the Bird, from his gray shadowy side.
This was her most dreaded stinky sticky chore.
A clothespin on her nose, she quickly scooped out the smelly mush.
Yuck! It made her totally want to scream and hide.

Little Mariah didn't much like the lonely work she did in the shack.

No one gave her a hand or talked to her,

just her mother's hypocritical bird, who only squawked back.

But there was one time unlike any other,

when everyone pitched in and helped one another . . .

CHRISTMAS TIME!

Mariah, her mother, and the bird would sweep, dust, and shake out the bugs.

They straightened out the pictures and scrubbed the filthy red rug!

They spruced up the windows and rickety rails with holly and fresh pine,

and polished the piano so good, it made the whole room shine.

Little Mariah hummed "Deck the Halls"

as she strung popcorn and cranberries

and taped paper snowflakes on the wobbly walls.

"Fa la la la la la," Mother La Diva joyfully chimed in,

and at Christmas Time, singing instead of talking wasn't weird at all.

As a matter of fact, Mother La Diva got quite festive,

putting hot cocoa in holiday mugs with marshmallows on top

and placing an enchanting Advent calendar on the piano, where chocolate treats

were hidden behind flippity flaps that flop.

Mother La Diva often left to sing for their supper,
leaving Little Mariah in the shack with no lock, alone and insecure.
One of the reasons Little Mariah loved Christmas Time so much
was because her mother was home a little more.
But one Christmas night, her mother went to the store to buy some candy canes,
and that's when double trouble hit the door.

In the grand white house high up on the hill lived a fancy family from France.

They spoke with odd English accents, which was weird,

but appeared pretty perfect at first glance.

The mother, father, brother, and sister all had piercing blue eyes,

plus a bunch of cats.

The parents were aloof, collectively the cats were smelly,

and the kids were brats!

The boy thought he was a rock star, though he couldn't play guitar or sing.
But he kinda looked like one. His hair was glossy blond,
precisely cut like feathers on a partridge wing.

He wore a denim jacket with buttons and skulls
with a hip band T-shirt underneath,
and in the back pocket of his crisp blue jeans, he kept a menacing comb
with very fine and sharp teeth.

The girl dressed in the cutest, newest clothes with light brown freckles that speckled her clean milky face.

She had fringe bangs and incredibly long straight golden hair that she swished, swooshed, and flippantly flipped all over the place.

The boy and the girl were bigger, cooler, and richer than Little Mariah
and secretly teased her about her shabby shack, hapless hair, and tacky tatters.
Most of the time, they wouldn't break her down
because she had her own special music and to her that's all that matters.

But this wintry Christmas night when Mother La Diva was out,
the boy and the girl burst into the shack and started to laugh and shout.
"Look at your silly cheap paper and popcorn decorations, and what's that ugly
calendar on your dumb piano all about?"

The boy whipped out his scary comb and glided it through his hair, and when he got near his ear, the teeth became fangs and whispered, "Go kick over that pitiful Christmas tree over there!"

The boy did as the comb ordered, giggling with such delight.

Then the girl flipped her long heavy hair and it whipped around the room like a

tornado, destroying everything in sight while Little Mariah shook with fright!

She scampered and took cover under the tiny kitchen table
and sang in a whisper-whistle to herself in order to feel stable.
The boy pointed his pointy comb at her and yelled,
"Little Mariah's song sucks; she's a little loser. Ha! That's her new label!"

"Little Loser! Little Loser!" chimed the sister and brother.
Little Mariah kept singing higher and higher,
hugging her knees with one hand and closing her ear with the other.

She peeped her head out,
and through the yelling and mayhem looked toward the window
and saw the lace curtains dancing.
But wait, what's really happening—could it be so?
Snowflakes were twinkling, flittering, and prancing!

"IT'S SNOWING!"

she exclaimed, her eyes twinkling bright.

"And I didn't even wish for snow on this Christmas night!"

Little Mariah scurried and grabbed her coat off the crooked hook, flung open the door, squealed, and swirled out into the night while nobody looked.

She ran and ran, letting the frosty fresh air kiss her cheeks
rosy to match her red coat
and the snowflakes catch in her haphazard hair
where they would glitter, glisten, and float.

She rushed through trees in the backyards of the big houses,
leaving all the chaos behind in the little shack,
and didn't stop until she was deep into the mysterious wild woods
before she even looked back.

She came upon a pristine clearing,

lay down on the sparkling, white soft blanket, her heart cheering,

and waved her arms and legs to make an angel of snow.

Underneath the stars, Little Mariah looked up into the dark sky.

The more she moved her little limbs, the more the stars started to grow and glow!

As the snow fell on her face and lashes, she blinked her eyes.
The next thing she saw, the stars turned into snowflakes
that looked like fairies that looked like butterflies!

Little Mariah broke out into a high-pitched song at the very sight.
The Snowflake Butterfly Fairies were luminous! Glorious!
And none of them looked or danced alike.

They pirouetted, cabbage patched, and boogalooed to her exquisite tune.
The trees, moss, mushrooms, all the woods began to bust a move—
even the dazzling full moon!

As the Snowflake Butterfly Fairies danced around,
fantastical ornaments flew from their wings
onto the trees made from snow scooped up from the ground.

From their sweet fairy breath,
they blew out silver garlands, glassy icicles, and magical crystals
decorating the gnarly limbs and pointy needles.
So enchanted by their beauty, Little Mariah followed the fairies.
As they flickered and flew, she twirled and tweedled.

The fairies flew faster, deeper into the woods and out of Little Mariah's sight.
She was lost and scared, surrounded by a daunting forest
and the dark darkness of night.

She aimlessly roamed between the big old trees.

Far off in the distance, she heard a deep murmur of cantankerous voices.

Little Mariah didn't know where she was,

so what were her choices?

The scary sounds grew closer and louder,
so frightened Little Mariah ran blindly as fast as she could,
until she stumbled and stubbed her toe
on what she thought was a piece of wood.

As she bent down to tuck her stocking back in the hole in her boot,
she touched a radiant, beaming heart-shaped stone.
It completely enchanted her,
so she hurriedly put it in her coat pocket and sang like a flute.

Before she knew it, she was encircled by a gang of bullies
in drab green uniforms and camouflaged in ice.
It was the notorious Shamey Shame Boys.
"BLAH! BLAH! BLAH!" they vehemently chanted at Little Mariah.
These boys were not at all nice.

They threw fireballs at the beautiful, wise old trees just to watch them burn.
The Shamey Shame Boys didn't like anyone who wasn't just like them.
Worst of all, they didn't like to read or learn.

Little Mariah was so terrified she took the stone out of her pocket,
sang, and held it tight against her chest like a locket.

A brilliant beam of light shot out of the rock and through her heart.
She followed the glow and all her fear disappeared. That was the best part.

The light stopped at a moist, mossy tree stump,
with a big, really old book sitting on top of it.

The cover was bedazzled, bejeweled, and in the middle a heart-shaped hole.

Still clutching the stone, Little Mariah put it in, and behold . . .

. . . a perfect fit!

The Shamey Shame boys caught up with Little Mariah
and as they began to blurt out a nasty "BLAH!"
they saw the magical book, and all they could say was *Ahhhhh*.
The vibrant light coming from her heart started to melt their hard ice.
What was revealed was that they were really just a group of fearful little boys,
and some of them were even made of sugar and spice.

Then the book opened, the pages flipped and flurried,
and out came diamond-dusted dust,
and the magnificent Butterfly Fairy Queen emerged from the sparkly gust!

She summoned the fairies and guided them
to gather all the gems and crystals on the ground
and spin them into a big ring to put on Little Mariah's head like a crown!

"For your perfectly pure songs from the heart,
I hereby declare you the Christmas Princess!"
the beautiful Butterfly Fairy Queen sang.
"Yasssss! Little Mariah is the Christmas Princess!"
shouted the boys gleefully, who were now a pretty colorful gang.

The Butterfly Fairy Queen led them all through the woods, with the fairies in tow,
back to the shack, which was now perfectly straight
and decorated with candles, every window aglow.

Mother La Diva and Pavarotti were on the porch,
each wearing a fancy red velvet Santa hat,
but what really made their ensembles festive
were their merry smiles, and nothing says Christmas more than that!

The golden piano came rolling outside.

The Queen beckoned Little Mariah to sit and play.

All of a sudden, the cats came down the hill on a perfumed sleigh.

She happily plucked *Ding, Ding, Ding, Ding, Ding, Ding, Ding, Ding.*

Then folks from the big houses came around to the shack to sing.

And everybody harmoniously got along

as they sang Little Mariah's joyous Christmas song!

All I Want for Christmas Is You . . .